This Is
Figure
Skating

For Dash, as always, and for the Shaughnessys:
Sarah, Kate, Sam, Dan, and Marilou, who is the wit of the family —M. B.

For Tess —J. O'B.

Henry Holt and Company, Inc., *Publishers since 1866,* 115 West 18th Street, New York, New York 10011

Henry Holt is a registered trademark of Henry Holt and Company, Inc.

Published in Canada by Fitzhenry & Whiteside Ltd., 195 Allstate Parkway, Markham, Ontario L3R 4T8.

Library of Congress Cataloging-in-Publication Data
Blackstone, Margaret. This is figure skating / by Margaret Blackstone; pictures by John O'Brien. 1. Figure skating—Juvenile
literature. I. O'Brien, John, ill. II. Title. GV850.4.B53 1995 796.91'2—dc20 94-45695

ISBN 0-8050-3706-3 First Edition—1998
Printed in the United States of America on acid-free paper. ∞
10 9 8 7 6 5 4 3 2 1

This Is Figure Skating

Margaret Blackstone
pictures by John O'Brien

Henry Holt and Company   New York

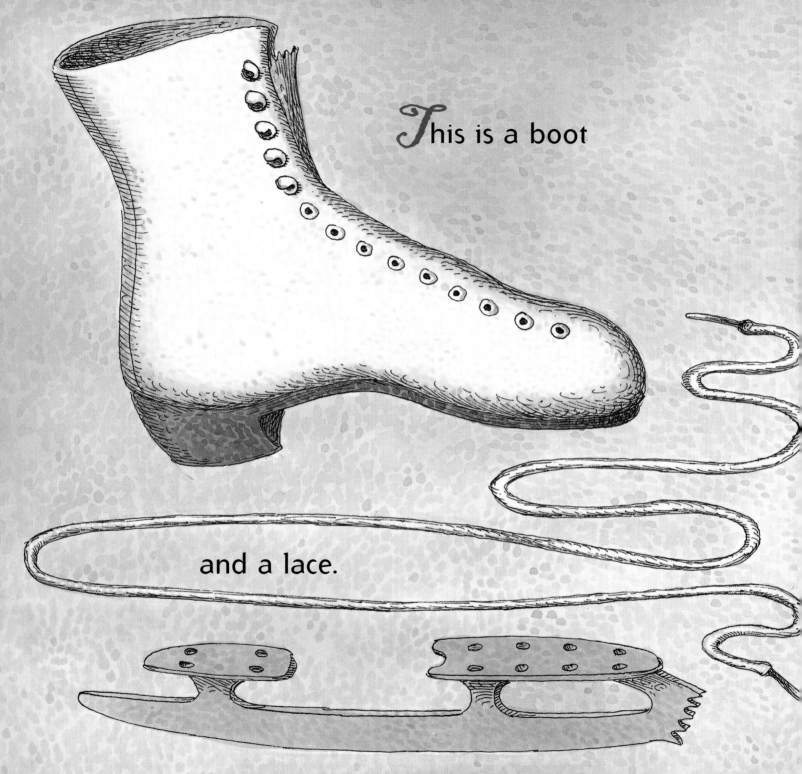

This is a boot

and a lace.

This is a blade.

This is a figure skate.

And this is a figure skater.

This is a rink.
And this is the ice
where the skaters glide,
fast and slow,
high and low,

forward and backward,

in circles

and straight lines,

figure eights

and serpentines.

This is called footwork.

Some footwork is fancy,

and some footwork is
used just to get there.

This is a jump.

This is a spin.

This is a sit spin.

This is a camel spin.

This is a scratch spin.
The skater spins so fast,
the blade scratches and scratches,
turn after turn.

These skaters can jump
and turn in the air

in a loop,

a double lutz,

and even a triple flip.

This skater can't jump.

But with practice and time
and some falls and some bumps,
he may turn around in the air—
three times, even four.

Skating is sport.

Skating is dance.

Blades click. Feet cross.
Arms fan. Heads toss.
Toe-picks dig.

A jig.
A jump.
A flying spin.

After skating all day,
there is a feeling that lingers—

cold feet, cold face,
a shadow of motion,
a speed that stays.

This is a figure skater late at night.
In her mind she's flying, she's fast.

A swoop and a glide,
an edge like a knife,
straight back,
arms curve,
hearts thump.

The highest jump.

The fastest spin.

A bow of grace.
She wins.

$15.95

DATE			